The Kule Tokwe Diaries

*

Collection of short stories

Hosea Tokwe

Mwanaka Media and Publishing Pvt Ltd,
Chitungwiza Zimbabwe
*
Creativity, Wisdom and Beauty

Publisher: *Mmap*

Mwanaka Media and Publishing Pvt Ltd

24 Svosve Road, Zengeza 1

Chitungwiza Zimbabwe

mwanaka@yahoo.com

mwanaka13@gmail.com

www.africanbookscollective.com/publishers/mwanaka-media-and-publishing

https://facebook.com/MwanakaMediaAndPublishing/

Distributed in and outside N. America by African Books Collective

orders@africanbookscollective.com

www.africanbookscollective.com

ISBN: 978-1-77928-409-9

EAN: 9781779284099

DISCLAIMER

All views expressed in this publication are those of the author and do not necessarily reflect the views of *Mmap*.

Foreword

This anthology of short stories resonates with the author's sharp rural experiences from early childhood and his present-day observations from the urban setting's daily struggles to survive. There are lessons to be learned from each and every story

Enjoy.

Contents

Part 1: Country-side Stories

Uproar at Chabwino Farm

The white farmer dressed in khaki shorts and a shirt dashed into the bank. A few minutes ago, he had locked a Daihatsu pickup after carefully parking it not far from the bank. Observing the look of his dressing, I was convinced he was coming from the farm, for the pair of farmer's shoes he wore was caked with brown dust.

Why was a white man up so early this morning? I was asking myself this question, for the streets of Harare were still empty this breezy Friday morning. My eyes darted towards his car once again. The pickup, though dusty, surprisingly looked in good condition. The wheels looked new. White farmers from distant farms made it a habit to drive weekly to purchase groceries and return to their farms. This particular white man's actions bore some mark of agency. I suspected he wanted to do his business and return to the farm sooner rather than later.

Moments after the white man entered the bank, a man emerged from nowhere. He was a short, middle-aged man. He wore long brown Revolution trousers, and beneath them protruded black, sharp-pointed shoes that glinted. I would believe he put on this clothing to cover up for his sinister deeds. An oversized, creamy jacket with torn seams gave him some airs.

Not long after, he crossed the road and beckoned his colleagues to come. They appeared immediately, and he waved his hand vigorously, urging them to move with urgency at the same time, pointing to the parked pickup car. His eyes glared at me once, and we exchanged glances. Was he about to hesitate? Satisfied that I was not interfering with their plans, he gave signs to his colleagues to locate in strategic positions. Resting his right elbow on a parking meter, he caressed his chin with his left hand. I watched all their schemes with suspicion. Once again, I turned my head, and this time our eyes met. Those red eyes spoke evil. I could tell he was susceptible to flaring up at the slightest provocation. When I lifted my eyes again, he was smoking a Shamrock cigarette. The revolting odour hit my nostrils, and I sneezed.

"Derek, get a wire fast," the other man urged his friend.

"Fine, take it easy, Domingo. I will look for one over the hedge", replied Derek as he hurriedly disappeared into the hedge.

From a municipal rubbish bin, Derek then collected an empty bean can, fastening the wire round it.

"Hey, be quick, act fast!" Domingo hissed as he lay underneath the pickup.

"Derek, come on, be a man," Domingo urged with a hoarse voice, his forefinger pointing to his wristwatch.

Domingo pulled the wire he was handed by Derek and hooked it underneath the pickup, making sure that the empty bean tin touched the ground. I watched the two accomplices do their act, the third man's gaze never leaving me. This was a highly calculated and orchestrated move.

Now the three accomplices' hands in pockets looked relaxed as they acted innocent, laughing and joking good-naturedly. From the bank's wide glass entrance, the white farmer emerged, a briefcase in his right hand. He gripped the handle, and the sharp knuckles stuck out with whiteness. He walked slowly towards his pickup. From where I stood, the man in dark glasses made the first move.

Taking off his glasses and acting innocent, the man walked silently towards the white farmer, passed him, and approached the tarred road. The white farmer opened the door and threw his briefcase on the passenger" s seat. Starting the engine, the pickup kicked up with a sound full of life. I could tell its engine was in good condition.

He reversed, hooting his car to warn one of the men who had stood behind the car. As he reversed, a queer sound caught his ears. The sound of a scrap of tin scratching the bare tar.

"Dammit, what the hell is this now?" The white farmer growled.

The car had sounded good when he left the farm, but now this strange sound had alarmed him. He had trusted this reliable and fuel-saving pickup all these years. He would bring fresh produce into the city to hand over to some bank employees, giving them packed carrots, onions, potatoes, and peas at giveaway prices. Now, was this pickup about to give him trouble? Should he check or drive on? Conflicting thoughts were troubling his mind. He reversed and brought the pickup back into a parking area.

"Check underneath the truck," one of the men urged, his forefinger pointing toward the pickup. The white farmer initially thought the man was joking, but upon further consideration, he decided to take a look.

"Yes, bass down, a wire sticking down there," he told him in perfect English.

The white farmer fell for the ploy! He went underneath. At that very moment the other man opened the passenger seat, opening the briefcase with a wire. In the blink of an eye, he had pulled off wads of bank notes and placed the briefcase back as if nothing had happened.

Emerging from beneath the pickup, the white farmer removed the wire and empty baked bean tin can that had been the source of all noise, throwing it away with a frown. He drove away immediately. Acting fast, the three accomplices had raced away into the alley.

Back at Chabwino Farm, farm labourers waited anxiously for the return of their employer from the city. They had worked hard for the past two winter months, defying the cold weather picking cotton.Now today they were getting their hard-earned reward, their two months" pay. They would be cause for joy and celebration in every household. At a nearby Tuck-shop, small bargains were being made already. Some were carrying their small groceries to their compounds, promising to return the following day with full payments.

"I can get, two more packets of kapenta and additional salt", the middle-aged woman grinned as she tried to balance the merchandise with her wrinkled arms.

Behind her Mariko Domingo salivated as he waited to collect his two "Shake Shake" Chibuku beer.

He had lost his wife three months ago and with no one to prepare his meal he just imagined caressing one Shake Shake to quench his thirst

Meanwhile some families huddled in their rooms were already enjoying their grocery of biscuits, bread and tinned foods driving away the urge they had endured to taste these items of food. But the more cautious ones held on to their food reserves.

"Three o'clock no sign of Bass from the road"

"Why!!" John Asante hissed.

"Let's bear with him. Maybe it might be the bad roads", his wife calmed him handing his favourite homemade mahewu drink.

Not long the sound of a roaring truck suddenly brought joy to the compound. Men, women and children streamed from their households murmuring excitedly. They were now milling around John Asante's compound with one thing in their minds, their two months' salary.

Meanwhile Mr. Schimdt, the white farmer brought his truck to halt. He had been happily humming a German song by one the popular pop singer but could not hold his bladder any longer. Stepping out from his seat he unzipped and relieved himself. Back on the seat he belched once again. He had taken a lot of beer, and there was dampness underneath his khaki shirt. First thing, a thought hovered in his mind, a light shower.

But wait, he checked on his briefcase and to his utter horror, the money was gone. His head was reeling with shock. He shook it vigorously

Now all the alcohol he had consumed was gone. Those men had played him the trick. How could he have been fooled? Three hundred meters away he could see the double story of his homestead. To the left he would pass through the compound before parking in front of his house. Why where the farm labourers milling for at this late hour? He was in big trouble. Could he reverse and drive back?

He started the engine and passing the crowded compound drove straight to his house. The family welcomed him back. A thought prickled him to enquire about the milling outside but he instantly dismissed it. He was hungry all he thought of now was a heavy meal. But this was not the right time. Suddenly his hands were shaking.

The faint sound of the gate at first seemed from a distance but grew louder. Then he heard his name being called. What?

With his pit bull behind him he was at the gate in an instant.

"What is this all about Asante?" he growled.

Asante opening the metallic gate, fought to control his shaking hands. The farm labourers had told him that they wanted their wages immediately without failure after he had failed to change their minds or they would burn the homestead. The chilling warning had sent Asante to the gate without him being given a chance to restrain them.

"You, you say they want to burn my homestead today, why, why, why, have I refused to pay them" The white farmer Schmidt hissed with anger.

His face had turned a pale red and he was shaking uncontrollably. He had not received such hair-raising threats before. He could not stomach these threats.

"Mr Schmidt, they, they say its two months with no wages", Asante managed a stammer.

Before Asante had finished narrating the message in full a crowd emerged holding glowing starks of burning grass. They were singing a peculiar liberation war song *Hondo yauya Zimbabwe* in Shona. Mr Schmidt thought fast, he raced back into the house to make the distress call, but it was too late.

The angry labourers had set the cattle pens alight and the cattle had broken gates and escaped in panic. There was pandemonium. Schmidt watched in horror at the unfolding events.

An hour later he heard the warning gun shots roaring. The police had arrived at the scene. The compound went silent. Who would be held responsible? Sitting on his wooden stool,

Mr Schmidt, face crestfallen, gave the police report. Upper most in his mind was an early trip back to the city to collect the wages so as to save his farm.

The dead man's possessions

Two days after the death of Musoni of Tandi Village, the situation at the homestead remained breathlessly tense. Yes, friends, relatives, former workmates, and church members had gathered together in their numbers, but a mystery still hung in the air, the dark family secret.

It was no wonder here and there the village folks spoke in hushed voices, for the question on everyone's mouth was, "Why had all of Musoni's children decided to stay?" It was a question whose answer nobody knew.

That other day the relatives had suggested the need for (a caucus meeting, but the siblings had flatly refused, and this left relatives in a state of trepidation. The siblings knew what they wanted to be done, so who were they to decide for them? But to these relatives, the isolated behaviour of every sibling led them to conclude that it was a matter of grave serious concern.

Ever since their childhood lives the four siblings had flourished. Each one of them had received a good education and attended reputable universities, both regional and abroad. Ultimately, they all entered the world of work and were influential figures in reputable companies.

Rodgers, the eldest of them, had flown all the way from Europe in time to attend the father's burial here at Tandi

Village. Francisco had laid the groundwork by organizing transport logistics, and with the assistance of his two sisters, and were going to engage a high-profile catering company. The villagers had feasted and eaten to their fill. Now that the funeral was over, who would reveal the family secret?

A day later, Rodgers, tall, dark, and of medium built, pulled his young brother Francisco aside, and in a matter of minutes they had been swallowed in the bush, some hundred meters away from the homestead yard. They were determined to keep the affairs of their inner family core from being a subject of debate and unnecessary wrangling.

Rodgers was the first to break the silence.

"The issue of our late father's secret possessions should be a strict family matter. Are we together, young brother?" Rodgers just gave his brother a wild stare.

"Do you hear me?" Rodgers shot the question with a slight, forward, menacing look.

Francisco the young brother's eyes almost watery with fear nodded his head, but imagining he would agree was a pipe dream. Being a religious family man and Deacon at one of the upcoming Pentecostal churches, he did not allow himself to be embroiled in partaking in the traditional approaches to resolving family mysteries.

"Mmmmm, no, no, no," Francisco raised both hands in surrender at last.

"Then you shall face the consequences, brother," Rodgers growled angrily like a provoked bull.

"The old man is not gone, but his spirit still hovers in the homestead. You do not want to listen to me; do not ever say I did not warn you." Rodgers raised his forefinger at Francisco as they headed back towards the homestead.

The elders stared at them questioningly, but none dared to question them about their secret short errand. The two brothers knew that Uncle Kerenge, with beady eyes and a short moustache, was not to be trusted. He could break loose and spit out every detail of information once his lips came into contact with the highly intoxicating African illicit brew. They passed him on their way inside the homestead's six-bedroom house.

"Auntie Tandi I have decided that we go it the traditional way", Rodgers announced moments after they had locked themselves inside the house.

"In that case I have no problem with that, my brother," the big sister concurred.

"Now whom shall we approach for the guidance for the ritual?" Big sister's question took them off guard.

Would it be wise to engage the headman and share with him the hidden family secrets? It was a tough matter to reveal, yet on the surface of it, they all knew no other alternative options.

After the siblings had narrated the family secret, Champion the Headman took a deep breath and swallowed the hair-raising revelation. He cupped his right palm on the cheek for a while longer. At last, he opened up.

"I hear you, my cousins; this is a very tough task in our hands," he nodded his head, his small eyes searching deep for their reaction. After lengthy deliberations, they all agreed to seek the Chief's approval to engage a spirit medium.

The chief's compound had a line of huts, but the newly white four-bedroom house stood out. All was quiet, and from a distance they went on their knees, clapping their hands in traditional fashion, the headman taking the lead, raising his voice to praise the chief's totem.

"What brings you here?" the Chief's messenger asked them.

"Young children cry for their home to be cleansed," the Headman replied.

"Then I will ask the chief to come first to hear your plea." The messenger retreated into the house.

The Chief having given his consent, the Musoni homestead the following day was sombre, with only traditional leaders in attendance. The witch doctor, barefoot and clad in animal hide, waved an animal tail, gesticulating in a strange language.

Standing in the centre of the homestead, he groaned, then, as if out of breath, went silent. Moments later he opened his porch and threw away some strange objects.

"Rodgers, show me the granary now!" shouted the witch doctor.

The siblings, who had been sitting together in one room, stared wildly at each other in alarm. Since their early childhood, they had heard strange, hair-raising child cries from the granary, but even their mother did not allow any of them nearby.

Now they gave Rodgers the eyes, and without hesitation he left the house. Outside, they could register the witch doctor groaning as if possessed by a spirit. What happened moments later sent heart-wrenching shivers. Strange and alien cries deafened the homestead.

Two owls, a rabbit, and a kitten, all dead, were brought before the Siblings. They all looked in awe, shell-shocked.

"That brown suitcase, that brown suitcase is breathing there," the witch doctor pointed at the late Musoni's bedroom.

"I will open the door," Francisco, the younger brother, volunteered.

"Stop! Don't you dare touch that! You will die!" The witch doctor pounced on the young man just before he had touched the suitcase.

"Give me the axe now!" the witch doctor demanded.

The witch doctor raised the axe and its heavy impact broke the door handle. The forceful nature of the execution sent the witch doctor falling awkwardly. He lay spread-eagled. Instantly, he went on all fours, crawling and wrestling with the brown suitcase.

"I got it, I got it," he shouted breathlessly. As the siblings watched the tense unfolding event the silence was equally breathtaking. What followed was even more stunning to the core. A strange, human-like goblin burst out, clutched in the witch doctor's hand. His hands were dripping with blood.

Somewhere inside his animal-skin hide, the witch doctor produced a sharp, homemade metallic knife that he drove deep into the goblin. He groaned, panted, and shrieked; his whole body bathed in sweat. All the eyes widened in fright at the flowing blood. This brought to finality the age-long-held family secret. Taking a deep breath and wiping the sweat off his forehead with the back of his hand, the witch doctor gave his last instructions.

"Do not open that sack. Tomorrow before the break of dawn, exhume your late father's grave and bury that sack", and with those words, the witch doctor left without uttering nothing more. The Siblings could do nothing but only stare at each other in amazement. For the first time there was an air of relief for at long last the dead man's possessions had been revealed opening a new chapter at the late Musoni's homestead.

Death at the dip tank

The heavy sound of an object hitting on the wooden door echoed in the young boy's eardrums in the middle of a dream. He sprang up instantly from the flat reed bed. He was breathless with shock and wonder. What could that have been? A little dazed, heart-pumping, he sat thinking deeply in the semi-dark hut.

Moments later, from a distance, he heard a faint voice, the voice of his mother calling him by his name, for Vance was his name. He remembered her telling him that his father had given him this name. Hurriedly, he scratched the bare cow dung floor, grabbing his shorts and torn brown t-shirt. Leaving the hut, barefooted, the young boy tip-toed towards his mother's hut.

"You have to follow the other boys to the kraal immediately and herd to the dip tank, big brother was here moments ago. You know him," his mother warned with a chilling voice.

Young Vance straightaway followed the footpath that directly led to the kraal. Vance, realising that after all it had not been a dream, but actually it being his big brother's heavy knock, he had to move faster.

Arriving almost breathlessly by the kraal, he felt the sudden chill of the early morning breeze but could do nothing about it save to chatter his teeth. There before him was the intimidating big brother. He just imagined how ferocious he had felt leaving the hut without receiving any response from him. Donning in an oversized khaki trench coat and putting on a monkey hat, he looked more like a madman who would scare the daylights out of an onlooker. His bloodshot red eyes were unwelcoming; they sent shivers down the young boy's spine. The young boy could not do anything about this threat.

The silence between them seemed endless but was broken by his loud sneeze in reaction to the strong, pungent odour of the cow dung that hit the young boy's delicate nostrils. Some mucus was sliding down his nose; he brushed it with the back of his hand.

The hoarse voice of Big Brother urging him to drive cattle to the dip tank brought the silence to an end. The young boy shouted in haste at the cattle herd, driving them out of the kraal. He had silently counted each, but soon lost interest; at most, he guessed them to be close to forty.

Driving their fathers' cattle to the dip tank was one of the pleasures that he enjoyed during school holidays. Today he was wondering why he was the only boy being coaxed to drive the herd, but moments later his face wore a broad smile as three other young boys joined them. The barking male dog, *Duty*, added to the spectacle, chasing after young calves that kicked their hind feet in the air. Big brother did not want the cattle to spread; he remonstrated with them to keep the cattle together and not let them gallop in different directions.

"Comb them, comb them," Big Brother urged them on. The young boys giggled, mimicking these words. It was great fun.

The cattle dip tank was located in a bushy area close to the farming area of Chimbwanda West; it was an old structure surrounded by a barbed wire fence. This dip tank was close to what were then known as Purchase Areas, where a few blacks owned large farms.

The strong smell of cow dung hovered in the air around the dip tank. The young boy and other boys of his age now stood guarding their herd as Big Brother submitted the stock card for inspection by the dip tank attendant.

Vance had never seen so many cattle herds, bulls, cows, and calves mixing and mingling as they trampled upon the bare ground. They were of different shapes, others with very long and sharp horns similar to the Masai breed from a country called Kenya. Sooner or later, they would plunge into the dip tank water.

The boys raised their heads instantly. What could have roused them to look in another direction? From afar the sound of a roaring bull had registered in their ears. They had also seen a change in behaviour from their young bulls, for they had ceased chasing around after heifers. They had been silenced by the loud roaring sound of the huge bull. The young bulls stood still.

The huge darkish brown bull came running with its sagging testicles almost scratching the ground. Its breath was almost audible as it puffed and bellowed, exhibiting its dominance.

Sniffing in the air, it ran around looking for cows and heifers, stopping once on an anthill, chipping soil with its sharp horns. The young boys who had experience of herding cattle for long, were aware of the behaviour exhibited by the bull. It was fancying for a challenger. Seizing the opportunity the young boys drove the other black hornless bull closer.

Both bulls came to a sudden clash of heads with sheer force, hoofing and puffing. Alarmed by the ferocity exhibited by the two bulls, the young boys scurried away and took to the trees, shouting with excitement. There followed total mayhem as the fighting bulls chased and pushed each other raising dust.

The young boy, Vance, hung on the tree branch. Earlier on watching the bullfight to him promised to be a spectacle, but with the fight heightening up, he saw the first traces of blood trickling down. His uncle's bull was bleeding from a deep cut on the neck. Then more blood and mucus emerged from the nose. What if the bull would die at this dip tank? Alarmed, the young boy thought of separating them. That was a risky option to take. He realized it later.

Suddenly, as if possessed, the black hornless bull withdrew a few steps and head-butted the other bull with full force. The hard blow stunned the other bull, sending it falling heavily. It was groaning as it endured more blows on its head.

Sensing the danger, Vance, the young boy, dropped from the tree and hid behind thick shrubs a distance away. He had initiated the bullfight, and now it had reached dangerous levels.

The duelling bulls could not be separated. From the corner of his eye, the young boy saw the other bull's eyes bulge, with some froth emerging from the mouth. It was staring at death. Thus, he heard the alarming distress call.

"The knife, someone get us a knife quick," the dip tank attendant shouted loudly "Please, the bull is wheezing out of breath." The urgency of the voice sent shivers down the boy's spine.

At this point in time there was no mistaking that he was realizing the gravity of his act. Soon they would search and find out the culprit.

The unfolding events were now no longer pleasing, the dip tank attendant and other cattle owners stood in a soberer mood while the thick-skinned man wearing a cowboy hat drove his sharp Okapi knife into the bull's carotid gland. It groaned, its hind legs kicking in the air, sending a few men scattering on the ground. That was the very last act. From behind it, the bull released cow dung and lay still.

The other cattle owners gave their hand in the slaughter, driving knives to the distended stomach. Breathless with shock, young Vance had witnessed what he had never seen in his childhood, a mass of internal organs exposed.

"Bring fresh tree branches, and keep the dogs away, please," the dip tank attendant cautioned the cattlemen The tree branches were cut to cover all internal organs, large and small intestines, liver, offal. Somewhere in the clear sky came a strange noise, the vultures. These birds of prey sensed the smell of a carcass from a distance away.

"Who is the owner of the black hornless bull?" The question stung the young Vance. Darting from shrub to shrub, the boy retreated deep into the bush, he did not want to be held accountable.

He was now retracing the way back home. Up in the sky, the sun shone, sending sharp rays to the bare earth. Running now, he followed a riverbed. At times he got lost in huge dungeons, but at this point his ears registered the sound of a laughing hyena. Tear drops of fear slide down his cheeks. He told himself that he was not ready to die. He was running for dear life now. Dusk was setting as he dug his heels into the ground, driven by the desire to avoid losing his bearings and failing to reach home.

Ahead of him he saw a winding footpath. Could this be the familiar one? He was running now, following it. He felt like a prisoner being pursued by armed prison guards with menacing dogs. Then he saw glowing embers of fire. The sound of a barking dog stopped him in his tracks. A familiar barking sound.

"No, Vance is not yet home." his mother's voice rang in the deep night from a distance.

"We are to report at the chief's homestead tomorrow," big brother's deep, hoarse voice announced regrettably.

Shocked, the young Vance crumbled to the ground, and beneath his ribcage he felt the fast thumping of his heartbeat. You are in trouble. He felt as if an echoing voice was drowning his ears. There was no other way out; he would face the consequences of his actions

A Night's Journey Home

I t is on a late Friday afternoon, an old pensioner and his son cross the busy road linking the old location and the industrial area. They both put on broad smiles, upon seeing the bus they had anticipated to carry them home. Their smiles even broadened further as they stared on the dashboard, at the written inscription visible in black and white.

"That one is our bus sonny, we are lucky," the old man had said pulling his son's thin wrist with urgency as they embarked into the bus.

Leaving the old Mbare Musika Bus Terminus the bus meandered through the vast expanse of the rural area taking them the better part of three hours to reach their final destination.

At long last the old Leyland bus grunted to a halt and the driver killed the engine. The lights were dimmed. The man's feet were first to land onto the pool of water.

"Aaaaaa", he suddenly cursed, shocked by the splashing water on his face and all his clothes. "Careful, careful", he warned his son before stepping to his side.

Now he held his son's hand as he sought their bearings. That night it had rained heavily in the countryside. They both could smell that scent characteristic of dry land welcoming the first patches of rain. The ploughing season was beckoning.

As they walked tracing their way home in the dark night, they could hear the fast fading and groaning sound of the ancient bus receding away. The bus crew were also getting close to the end of their journey at the local township. Sooner or later the sound of the bus would be inaudible.

"Stop!" the man said to his son. In the dark, he fastened his farmer's shoelaces after he had landed in a large puddle of water. The old man, whose clothing had already gotten wet and damp, shivered slightly from the night's humid air. Had they guessed the correct direction of their destiny. It was a matter of instinctiveness. Night times like these were not good to walking at night in the countryside especially after the rains. Ancient beliefs in the African society forbade walking in dark after falling rains for it was during these weird hours that nocturnal sounds abounded. A sacred myth being that ghosts would leave their graves to feel a breath of fresh air.

"Aaaaah," the man cried nervously

"What is it father? Is something wrong?"

"Shhhh, keep quiet." His voice trembled

"You want to say something father?"

The man's mind brought to memory an incident where a man was whacked a heavy slap by a ghost, fortunately the man in the story had lived to recount the incident. He held his breath awhile.

All was dark, silent and dull around them and the man had a tearful feeling. If the boy had moved close enough to his father, he could have heard the loud thumping of his heart. His father was already in state of panic.

"I said keep quiet, am saying this for the last time. Do you hear me?"

Suddenly a fire lit in front of them. The boy saw it first and ejaculated, "Father, look at that fire!" It momentarily disappeared and appeared again this time intense and brighter as if some people were warming themselves.

Suddenly the old man jerked his son away from the direction, but still the fire appeared in front of them.

While the boy felt fascinated, the man was feeling numb and trembling.

A worried expression came over his face. Quite vague visions clouded his mind. No, they could not oblige him to change his faith. He could not allow dark thoughts to overpower him.

"Let's stop here now. Kneel here." The man said between his breathe.

They both knelt down and he began to pray. He was beseeching the Lord to guide them from evil and to light on their way. He was talking about the troubles they had gone through right from the city; all encounters they had experienced along the way and, now this trouble. The man pleaded with the Father in Heaven for their destiny. As he prayed emotionally it compelled him to weep and to mutter incoherent words. Next came a thought that made him wince and mutter incoherently once again.

"We can walk home now my son." the man finally said and they rose from the ground. The boy now behaved with dignity towards his father.

For twenty minutes they walked silently. The glowing light did not appear. Miracle!

Half an hour later the boy wanted to piss. The man waited as he did so. Then they both heard the whistling sound. A blanket of silence enveloped them.

This time the old man felt his hairs rise. Who would be whistling at them at this hour of the night? It was drizzling once again and their feet splashed in the puddle of water on the ground as they resumed their journey. The sound helped distract them and they made steady progress towards home.

After some time, the man saw huge silhouette figures. From village to village runs a road that cuts through gum trees. Those should be my tall gum trees, he thought to himself. He gripped his son's hand as they increased their pace. Only now he was sure that this was the right way towards home.

By now the son was quiet, could it be that he was growing tired or possibly not sure when they would reach home?

At last, the man's shaking hands collided with the hinges of the metallic gate. In the dark a wide grin spread on his face, a triumphant smile that overcame his earlier fears. Fearing the unknown, a mixture of tears and mucus mingled flowing on their downward journey past his big black lips and finally to the chin with a new crop of grey beard coming up.

"Joel we are home now." This was the first time to call his son with his first name. Now his eyes were not deceiving him. Those tall gum trees swaying sideways following the whims of the wind were the ones he had planted two decades when he arrived to settle on this piece of land. Father and son had no worries, they were home at long last. In the dark night the old man giggled good naturedly almost sending his son comatose with laughter. In his mind he could now picture his family enjoying the goodies.

"We are home sweet home Joel" the old man remarked excitedly as they laughed their way home under the bathing rising summer moon.

Tales of the Makorokoza

The pick handle slid from Gijima's sweaty palms clattering away a few meters from where he stood. All this happened suddenly and unexpectedly. His eyes took on a wide strange look. Talk of luck. He could have cried, a cry of joy, but he restrained himself. Momentarily, he felt as though awakening from dream but soon realized that it was not as he had thought. No, his eyes were not deceiving him for there, right in front of him, he had struck gold, real pure gold after many months of painful toil.

He stood there erect like a statute. In this exhilarating state of mind, a wild thought had suddenly visited him. It struck the centre of his head. This is your gold a voice was playing words in his head and no one should lay claim on it. It seemed like a strange ancient voice instructing him now. Casting his glance at the glittering gold once again so many wild options of hiding the gold were flooding in his fast-thinking mind. He was also feeling the itchiness of his body as dump sweat clung to his dark soiled t-shirt. It seemed he could hear a shouting voice; "This is my gold this is my gold," echoing in his ears. And beneath his ribcage he felt the rhythmic drumming of his heartbeat. "Act now!!" The pumped-up adrenalin urged him on. Now he was no longer himself but behaved as if a strange devil incarnate had visited him. The greediness that had seized him brought a new wave of bravery.

One would ask was the daring feeling gripping him worth the risk he was about to take. He had decided to throw caution to the wind.

One option he thought was to chip the gold and hide it inside many pockets of his oversized muddy corduroy trousers before finding a secret escape route. Shrugging his shoulders, he reflected on the fatal risk he was about to take defying his conscience. The Makorokoza game was fraught with risk, he knew it very well, for it was a matter of life or death. A friend could be a dangerous enemy at the spar of a moment.

Gijima lifted the rusty shovel from where it laid, deciding on his next move. Gijima!! Was that his name being called? He had been stopped in his tracks, and cupping his right ear listening intently, he registered the echoing sound of his name being called. How the sound had penetrated through the caves and twisting tunnels in this old disused mine. This did not only surprise him but haunted him. It was terrifying as if like coming from a living ghost.

Shocked out of his guts he stood listening in case his ears were deceiving him. The beads of sweat on his farrowed forehead were accumulating fast. The veins on his arms where visible as he tightened his fist gathering courage.

Someone had told him long back that striking gold was no mean feat but an answering call from the ancestors. Meditating over it he almost felt tears gathering in his eyes. Overcome with emotion, Gijima fell on both knees trembling to the ground. He stopped suddenly feeling as though his ancestral prayers had been interrupted by an invisible being.

A soiled sack that he had at one point used as a bed rest lay a few metres away. Frantically with an act of urgency, he was now at work, chipping the gold. Gijima shivered with excitement as he worked. It did not take him long. With the sack perched on his shoulder he searched for an exit route. All along he could hear voices and sparks of searching lights. They were coming after him, they were smelling blood. Yes, the Makorokoza way to riches was a game of spilling blood.

Turning his head sideways he went for the dark tunnel. As he stepped into the unknown, his feet splashed on water, then as he stretched his hand, his heart leapt. Could he have touched a human being? He nearly let out a cry of anguish but quickly held himself stiff and remained composed. Not now Gijima, a voice was telling himself. Yet as he moved it seemed he was falling into a deep pit of darkness. Twice thrice his feet buckled and he fell to the ground. Were those eyes? How could one see? No! He nearly shouted but held himself again. The gold. Yes, he could feel the weight of the precious gold on his painful shoulder. He was thinking of his fate now. What could happen to him, his family and their welfare for right now he was being tracked. They wouldn't be fooled. But it was his gold thus why right now he was heading home.

When he saw the light, his eyes almost went blind. He brushed his eyes with the back of his right-hand leaving grains of soil that made his eyes itch. An idea came to him. No one should see him. Checking his bearings he went for the forest, not on twos but fours. Yes, he had to crawl. It was hurting but it was worth the agony. Neither today nor the day after should he be home. He knew the Makorokoza way, he had to fool them.

For five days he stayed burrowed in a hole and at the entry he covered it with dry grass. Soon hunger took its tall. What could be the next move? Gijima's mind thought fast. Five days had been a long time, would he at long last take the risk. Dusk was setting in. He checked his bearings before emerging like a nocturnal animal. Today he was herding home. In the dark amid the jarring thorns, he found his way to his home.

At a distance he thought he saw a glowing light. Gradually drawing nearer thus when he registered the sound of beating ceremonial drums. He stood almost collapsing. Noooo! That was not his home, but the closer he advanced the louder the drums echoed with a strange welcome. He began to panic.

Indeed, as his face shown on the glowing lights the villagers ran to embrace him with comfort. But there was nothing to comfort, he lay there half dead.

The men lifted him into his hut close to the fire. He was powerless and his body had shrivelled. When he heard the tragedy, he half fainted again and they had to poor water. His true friends all because of gold had slaughtered his family in cold blood. The way of the Makorokoza, a terrible menace that had hit the country was already haunting Gijima. The blood of each and every family member wound be avenged.

"I will kill them, I will kill them", he hallucinated before going silent once again.

Joachim's soul returns home

The sweltering October heat wave is sweeping through the dense forest. The grass is slowly dying as the sun sucks every last drop of moisture out of the land. Trees, animals and man will all have to endure another few weeks of this blistering heat before the onset of the life-giving rains. Amid the maze of low tree branches, mostly thorny and leafless, a young girl makes her way through the undergrowth. She moves gingerly on her toes, mindful of hidden thorns and jagged stones protruding from the ground along the faint pathways. Her torn dress is a shade blue with faded yellow seams. With both hands she wraps it close to her light body in case hocked thorns might hold it back. She knows she has got to fetch the firewood for her mother who awaits at home.

All morning, she recalls, they had been pounding the grain, so now it is time for their first meal. Looking tired and weary the girl wipes beads of sweat on her forehead. She stops, corking her ear. Not very far away she registers the occasional whistling of lively hornbills somewhere among the trees, perhaps the males calling out for mates.

The forest is still, suddenly a voice breaks the silence. Her heart leaps, she holds back her breathe. There in front of her wide eyes, she stares in awe at a heap of firewood covered with rotten leaves. She hesitates. What could it have been? A voice within her asks. From that spot she hears a strange voice urging her to hold her nerve. Again, instructively an overwhelming urge to retrieve from the pile a dry termite-infested piece of wood seizes her. Then she hears the strange voice speak directly to her, stopping her instantly in her tracks. The sound of the voice is unmistakable.

"Thank you, young girl," the raspy voice says.

"Now my spirit can rest," the dead man's voice calls out again. It breaks the pervading silence.

She stands rooted to the spot, shocked and immobilized. She feels the hairs on her head rising. She registers the pounding heartbeat beneath her ribcage, mirroring her fear and bewilderment. All of a sudden like a cornered animal with no way of escape, she stands erect. Her wandering eyes now rest on the termite-infested piece of wood that she just drops in panic. She stares at it trembling, mesmerized by this kind of mystery.

"I know that you are afraid young girl, but fear not," the voice says, then pauses, before continuing. "From this day onwards, you are my guardian angel," says the dead man's voice quite distinctly.

"My name is Joachim Gurupira. Yes, Joachim is my name. I come from the village of Chinete in Musana." The voice is like a distant echo in her ears.

Though deeply unfathomable, it suddenly became clear to her that the small mound of earth on which grass had grown over the years, was a grave - Joachim's grave! Without doubt, the voice was coming from there. His remains had been lying there for twenty years. Twenty years had gone by since the late comrade had breathed his last. That was what the voice calling out said to her. And suddenly, like a vision, she could see it all in her mind's eye.

Twenty years back, on that fateful day, the dying comrade had looked at his blood-soaked denim shirt and known that the end had come. An enemy bullet had found its target in him, penetrating and lodging itself in his body. There was no point shouting for help. What life was left in him oozed out with the blood as his comrades retreated from the barrage of automatic gunfire, leaving him to his fate. Beads of sweat stood out on his brow and the damp patches edged with a salty whiteness under his arms grew visibly as he strained to undo the belt on his corduroy trousers.

As Joachim sat there waiting for the end, visions of his parents floated before his eyes.

"You will be free, yes, you will be free," he said. "You will enjoy milk and honey," he added to his words.

"I am gone now, but remember me-e-e-e-e!!!" the last words trailed off and his voice was barely audible.

With his life fading, he somehow achieved a new awakening and frantically brought out a James Version pocket bible from his back pocket. For some moments his mouth was agape. The words would not come.

Finally, he said, "God Almighty accept me in your Kingdom," and lay still.

The left corner of his eye was the last part of his body to see the fading glow of the setting sun. They happened together, his death and the setting the sun. He winced once and felt himself drifting into other worlds. His remaining strength ebbed away and he lay still. The bazooka, his unfailing companion all those years, lay next to him on the hard ground.

Joachim's body remained untouched, the soldiers had arrived on the spot and stood in awe.

Using the hoes collected from villagers, the soldiers frantically dug a hole then lifted Joachim's body into the grave. One soldier knelt a few meters from the fresh mound of soil and prayed before his mates buried the departed man.

That same spot, these many years later, was the very spot from where the voice of Joachim proclaimed the desire to return home, the home of his ancestors.

The voice pleaded with the girl encouraging her at the same time.

Joachim had joined the war in his early teens. It had happened on that dark night when the young adolescent was coming back home from the local township. The freedom fighters took him into the bush. He vanished without the chance to say farewell to his kith and kin. The political orientation and the guerilla war training in time transformed the boy into a freedom fighter.

Then followed ten years of ragged existence in a bitter guerilla war to unshackle the people from colonial bondage. Joachim had fought gallantly, but failed to see the dawn of freedom. His day of reckoning came when he least expected it.

For twenty years he had lain buried in the forest where wild beasts roamed and nocturnal animals thrived. Today his wondering soul had found hope, hope in the form of a young girl out to fetch firewood for her mother's hearth.

"Now, when you meet my people, tell them that Joachim wants to come home and rest." The girl winced. Was this truly happening to her? She was running back home wildly, all the time recalling the words.

"Mother, Mother Joa- Joa - Joachim," she stuttered once more.

The shocked mother gathered the villagers to what had become of her daughter's voice. A male strange voice pleading to rest in peace. The rituals were performed by the spirit medium and the Gurupira clan prepared to welcome the young girl. The reincarnation of Joachim their son.

Two days later, the Gurupira homestead was a hive of activity. The sprucing, the clearing of paths and tidying-up of the home was followed by the slaughtering of beasts. The women at the fireplaces stood at the ready to welcome the young girl.

The dressed in all black like a spirit-medium held everybody's breath. All black she led a group of her people towards the Gurupira homestead.

"Our son returns now, clear the way," a male voice uttered. The silence was breathtaking. Villagers stood in awe; some could be heard murmuring.

Barefooted, the young girl led the way silently and suddenly a sombre mood descended on the homestead.

"Bring all the gifts before the young girl sets foot inside the compound yard", a loud elderly male messenger voice echoed from a distance away from the homestead's periphery.

From nowhere a cloud of dust rose as muscular men dragged two beasts, a goat and three live fowls to the foreground amid whistling and ululation from the womenfolk.

The dust settled and silence descended once again. Step by step the young girl set her foot. For an entreaty she stood motionless, a hundred eyes feasted at her, this solitary and strange figure that held every soul's breathe motionless in the centre of the homestead. Then she did something that sent the young, the old and crawling, holding their mouth.

"Joachim sends me here with a message," she proclaimed.

Shocked, speechless, amazed and some in tears they waited with almost palpable anticipation.

"Hear me again. Joachim Gurupira wants to come to be buried here amongst his folks, I will not waste your time; I will lead you to collect his bones where they are buried." Her little speech done, she retraced her footsteps and led Joachim's people to where he lay.

In a matter of days, the Chinete village was thronged by all sorts of visitors: chiefs, headmen and councillors. Voices of joy, emotion and excitement rose as gyrating villagers went through their rituals. Some women swept all the pathway to the grave amid loud traditional religious songs in the choking dust.

At long last Joachim's remains had come back home to be reunited with his people.

The marriage day

The year is coming to an end on this windy Saturday morning. From the east dark black clouds float, obscuring vision of the sun's light, time and again. One wonders whether these are signs of an approaching winter.

Bostock turns his head towards the sky. However, what intrigued him was the sensation he felt as the chilly wind caressed his chicks. He smiled to himself, good naturedly.

Just after a few minutes back he had dropped off from the haulage truck by the main tarred road. It had been heading to Bulawayo, Zimbabwe's second largest city. Looking ahead he cast his eyes at a footpath snaking through the vast landscape of the grasslands.

A distance away his eyes caught sight of a large herd of beef cattle owned by the new farmers in these grasslands of Somabhula. Was it not some forty years back when white Commercial Farmers had owned this land? He mused.

That was not his worry right now. Instead, he allowed his somewhat tired eyes to marvel at the cattle herd, lazily nibbling at the grass flickering their ears. Bostock momentarily stopped to tie the loose shoelaces now completely damp from the evaporating morning dew. An uncharacteristic frown swept across his oily face, he had reached a decision, to start on the journey through the veld.

Now his eyes stared towards the landscape. There have been several veld fires this year, but thank God for the life-giving rains, the flora and fauna now flourished once again adding more beauty to the landscape. Even the few trees shown a new breath of life with tree branches swinging gently and sideways following the whims of the wind. Slowly, Bostock allowed his feet to lead the way towards a homestead

Today his neighbour's daughter was getting married. It has been but only a few months that Old Mureriwa had hastily started building a four-roomed house, but strangely, Bostock wouldn't have imagined that his neighbour was doing this to welcome his future son-in-law. After receiving the invitation to be one of the guests', things had changed, Bostock decided to attend the ceremony. Just a few days back unanswered regrets had tormented his mind. Why were all his daughters failing to get married, he wondered. Just recently the youngest daughter had fallen pregnant. This was the last stroll that had almost forced him to ignore the invite.

"Father to Matilda, my husband, it happens- just go," his wife had persuaded him but she herself could not imagine being the talk of the gathering because of her wayward daughters.

Let them enjoy the 'Roora Day', she miserably concluded as she urged his husband to go maintain relationships.

So many people were now breaking with the past old age Shona tradition whereby only few relatives would attend

'Roora Day'. Embracing this Western life style of "Roora Day" has become a showpiece of marriage.

Workmates, neighbours, relatives and church members all gathered to make merry and partake in food, drink and getting drunk. So today Bostock found himself amongst the teeming guests.

Arriving alone and unobserved Bostock passed through the open and inviting gate. There he observed a huge tree and behind it the cattle kraal. A few state-of-the-art cars including a police truck were parked beneath this tree. A lot was happening meriting the day's occasion. Some men had already killed and skinned a goat and were now laying a goatskin on a stone. One angry man kicked a dog hard on its hind leg before it attempted to lick the goatskin. It run away barking loudly as a result of the pain scaring a few women sending them scattering. This was just but one isolated incident. A few metres away women with Chitenge cloth wrapped around their waists attended to fires as they rolled huge cooking sticks preparing thick porridge, a favourite meal at these traditional functions. Young women not to be outdone were busy cutting chunks of meat and offal, placing them all in huge pots balanced on top of burning firewood.

One elderly man with white moustache sat on black plastic chairs chattering. Bostock stooped closer to him and as per African tradition he knelt down clapping both hands with dignity.

'The say the expected future son-in-law is yet to arrive so nothing happens before he pays the lobola", the old man with greying hair suddenly uttered the remarks.

Bostock raised his eyebrows wondering whether he deserved hearing this information.

There were three white tables surrounded by white chairs. Then there in the centre stood a small oblong shaped table with silver vases at each end. Yet again Bostock's face glowed with a smile as he imagined the exact chairs where the future son-in-law and future wife would occupy. So, they had chosen red and white colours, the English colours as they are known as the primary colours.

Big red and white blown-up balloons bounced around big poles adding to the beauty of the occasion.

"We kindly urge you to lift your chairs and occupy that place below the big thorny tree, you will enjoy the refreshing shade", a man dressed in navy blue suit announced his face taking on a kindly smiling look.

Could it be that the son-in-law had arrived. It was everyone's guess, and this confirmed it. Men in suits emerged from a twin cab clapping hands in unison as they entered the four-roomed house.

"It's them, the son-in-law's entourage. They have arrived to pay the bride price", giggled the toothless man who a while ago had been breaking silly jokes leaving men in stiches.

Now as the sons-in-law went through their marriage rituals men in groups chattered, some talking about those old days when white farmers with large tracks of land would breed quality beef cattle to be exported to EU countries.

Another group sat a few metres away engrossed in stories of their hunting exploits in the countryside.

"They are coming now", a voice uttered suddenly. Bostock turned his head in surprise. His expectation was summed up for his neighbour's daughter and her bride team come out of the house singing and rejoicing.

"The bride price has been paid, they are excited", a mischievous looking middle-aged man hissed into Bostock's ears.

The pervading odour of draught beer smelt from the man's toothless mouth. Bostock's lips pouted with disgust. At this instant he could only but just imagine if he would have been at the high table to avoid such incidents.

Suddenly all was quiet once again as the Master of Ceremony read through the programme of the day. Meanwhile a younger man passed around handing over leaflets of the programme amongst the seated invited men and women.

Prayers were conducted and then introductions and speeches followed. Bostock sat and reflected once again lost in his thoughts. He is imagined himself with his wife and daughters back home but he frowned at the thought and a thick lump nearly blocked his throat almost forcing him to momentarily loose his breathe. He lamented inwardly at the misfortune in his household. Then an evil thought manufactured in his mind. What if the two couples terminated their marriage vows suddenly in front of the marriage officer? He shook off this horrible thought vigorously.

"Ladies and gentlemen today we witness the joining in matrimony of this boy and girl", the ululation and whistling that followed awakened Bostock from his slumber.

After giving a lengthy speech, the marriage officer exhorted the bride and groom to honour their marriage vows in true faith and concluded with a touching prayer. The pomp here reflected a mini wedding, Bostock thought loudly. He was now seeing the new couple exchanging rings and their marriage vows. A women stood aside, maybe that is the aunt, Bostock surmised. His heart nearly skipped a bit as the woman missed hitting the cake within few inches.

Suddenly a wave of an appetising odour of delicious meal, beef, chicken and freshly cooked sausages pervaded the area. Has this been the time Bostock has all been waiting for? He followed the small queue religiously. There was everything from rice, traditional dish of rapoko, fresh lettuce, cucumber, green pepper and boiled potatoes. People ate and made merry as each and every one got lost in their own full plate.

Then something happened, sending the gathering laughing, for a dog pulled a plate from beneath a chair and as the middle-aged man wearing a faded suit attempted to stop he dog tripped and fell. Bostock had the last laugh that echoed and triggered more laughter.

The planes of the vast grassland were now experiencing the fading glow of the sinking sun. Everybody was in a merry mood. The drowning voices of invited guests made everybody feel at home. Bostock spoke into the ear of the short elderly man before dashing to Blair toilet.

"Group photo, group photo everybody!!" The master of ceremony hastily announced. Everybody gathered at the kraal, to pose for all important photos as is the traditional custom in these communities.

'I will kneel in front the bride and groom', Bostock came back shouting. As he tried to touch the bride, he lost balance and fell at their feet much to delight of men and women. Unfortunately, he landed on fresh cow dung. Would he wipe it off? There was no time for that now.

'We are leaving now'

'Anyone herding to Gweru?' a couple announced.

Bostock moved briskly towards double cab. He looked back for the last time at the venue of the marriage day. Reflecting with joy, he put on a good-natured smile imagining once again for how long this new family would hold together.

Part 2: Urban Stories

Hustling: A daily struggle in Harare

Piyo threw away the blankets from his springy bed alarmed by the intense brightness of the light inside his room. He hurriedly put on his black track suit bottom with yellow stripes and a grey t-shirt. Retrieving his dirty canvas shoes underneath the bed he cursed himself for failing to catch the early morning transport.

He stared at his reflection in the mirror, and lamented seeing himself putting on the same soiled clothes once again. How demeaning, he thought to himself but there was nothing he could do to improve his outer appearance. Why bother, the populace had become an impoverished lot and dressing has become less formalised in this struggle of hustling. Life moved on.

Piyo stretched his arm to check his wrist watch once again. He was already late and all the blame fell squarely on his shoulders.

As he stood up, he momentarily reflected on the long journey that he had travelled. It was a journey of hardship in a country whose economic meltdown he knew full well had become talk of the region.

Since completing his higher secondary school studies, he had neither secured a place at any of the local Universities nor could he afford the demanding fees pegged in foreign currency. His mother, despite being a government worker holding a good civil service position had openly advised him that she could not afford the tuition fees. That he could not secure university education became a reality, henceforth he decided on posting his applications and curriculum vitae to different companies but all in vain. This irked him. What did the future hold for him now, he wandered? Thus, one day he met an older schoolmate who advised him to order trinkets for resale in the city centre.

"Jeffrey, do you think this will work out", Piyo had sought for assurance from his friend.

"Mumm yaah" Jeffrey had mumbled figuring the best way to win his friend.

"You can give it a try for two months and come back to me", Jeffrey assured his friend his searching eyes gazing at him.

Piyo shied away nodding his head good-naturedly more out of acknowledging his friend's encouragement.

As they enjoyed their food at this Chicken Inn outlet Piyo listened attentively to Jeffrey's sojourn to Dubai as he recounted the several trips that he had taken to secure orders for bales of clothing, and different types of trinkets. There was the hustling to secure visa and last-minute air ticket purchases and flight bookings. Dubai to most people in African countries had become the gateway to the Middle East countries. The big business people were now into trading in fuel from some oil producing countries capitalising on political connections.

Piyo had listened to his friend imagining how great it would be to one day seize the opportunity to fly out to Dubai.

"Piyooo!" The calling voice from his clouded head suddenly brought his senses to the present situation.

A distance away, an idling high roof commuter omnibus had been calling for the last passenger. Piyo jumped in a few moments before it took off at this popular intersection of the neighbourhood location. As the speeding commuter omnibus headed towards the bridge, Piyo raised his eyes to get a better view of the landing airline. No, this was not the Emirates Airlines he had thought of but the South African Airways preparing to land on the Airport runway. Each time they passed adjacent to the runaway a piece of his mind always reflected on the Dubai story.

Fumbling his pockets he felt for his torn purse. For a fraction of a second his heart leapt with panic, but he relaxed moments later. In haste he had thrown the purse inside the plastic paperback that he now held on his lap. So, with a light smile he pulled a dirty United States one dollar note and forwarded it to the conductor. He expected for his change but when nothing was handed to him, he frowned in disgust.

Now in the city, he weaved his way through the mass of human traffic gritting his teeth with anger at the obstructing people all driven to the city by the quest to survive. Shoulders brushed on strangers, rushing feet stamped on each other with few mumbles of apologies here and there.

On the intersection the overwhelmed traffic officer had to summon all bags of tricks to control the mass of early morning traffic.

Piyo's mouth went agape upon realising that his selling post was now already occupied. A young lady had already spread her wares and held a familiar frizzy drink to her mouth. Stamping both feet in frustration Piyo waited agonisingly for the late arrival of Mr Patel to open his shop from where he had left his trinkets the previous day.

Around him tongue lashing voices echoed as they competed in an effort to win customers. Individualism had gripped the young men, women and the elderly as none could be left out in an effort to survive. "The Cult of the Hustle", broadly centred on being one's boss had addicted all the populace through motivation from the family, church and community to thrive and become the next generation of the new entrepreneurs. Piyo pouted his lips shaking his head for to his learned mind these were just but groans of poverty that had gripped his countrymen. Street vending had become a dog eat it dog affair.

Where was Mr Patel, Piyo wondered as his eyes grew pale with frustration? As he checked his wrist watch slowly ticking away he regretted not having asked for Mr Patel's contact details. Meantime his ears could only register the loud echoing voices each with its own persuading tune.

"Municipal police!" A piercing voice raised the alarm. Piyo reacted with a sudden dash. Street vendors with heavy wrapped cloth strapped on their shoulders, ran in different directions leaving a trail of trinkets and fruits strewn in the tarmac. A municipal open truck swept past loaded with heavily armed guards with rubber baton sticks. They were on the hunt after the street vendors. In such situations informers also posed grave danger. Not long a bystander shouted to alert the loaded truck.

"In the hardware store," he pointed in the direction.

The truck began to reverse. Piyo observed the truck, as the baton stick wilding police drew closer to the entrance. He was hiding behind wooden doors pretending to be a buyer. A mind chilling panic seized him; the moment the police entered the hardware.

"Where are the street vendors you are hiding here", the huge man putting on a cap roared as he headed towards the counter.

"Fish him out before all hell breaks loose here", he hissed

Being arrested and jailed were Piyo's least regrets that would dash his hope for securing university scholarship in future. He had to act fast. Pipping on an opening, he sneaked through by chance running through a passage towards the back door. That was his salvation. Bursting through, he found himself in dirty alleys. Together with other street vendors who had hidden their wares in garbage, they made haste to escape. Piyo kept on running twisting and turning ending up at the railway station.

There was a big man-made hole at the centre of a diamond mess perimeter fence. He passed through it easily then tip toped through past a junk yard, then by the dry riverbed. From there his ears once again registered sounds of groaning buses on their way into the city. Far from the madding crowd of daily street hustling Piyo felt relieved. He had only one idea, and he made up in his mind, to return to back home safely.

Street Raid

"**H**ey Banda, will you lead the team?"
"

"Yes Senior!" The huge man responded, spontaneously, with a trembling voice.

A good two metres tall of height and putting on a size ten pair of black safety shoes, Sergeant Major Banda stood upright at attention. His wide shoulders held a pair of big arms and not to be outdone, his bull-like neck secured a rotund shaved head. Meanwhile, his dark avaricious eyes hooded under stringy eyebrows were quietly traveling in circles and at one point resting on the numerous certificates and accolades hanging loosely on the walls of the Superintendent's Office. He swallowed up with envy.

"Have you heard me, huh" the Superintendent authoritative voice shot with venom, bringing back Banda to his senses. Banda stood at attention.

"Three months Banda, three months, tell me? Are you sure three months has elapsed without any street raids huh? What is your problem, tell me what is your problem?"

Today he could sense that his Senior was very upset and wanted results. This sudden outburst of anger from his Senior had shaken him. These were not routine orders but serious instructions to take real action. As he listened, he was breathing heavily, a faint whistling sound barely audible inside his chest. It sent negative messages to his brain, particularly the fear of losing his job.

That is why right now he was telling himself not to dare open his big mouth. The situation being tense, he dared not let it degenerate into harsh exchange of words, he would risk being fired on the spot.

He calmed down now that Senior's voice had subsided. Relax, a voice within warned him. He was cautiously aware of his high position, the position of Sergent Major. This to him was a most prized job that went along with an office, though small.

No! He should never lose this job. What would happen to his three-month old pregnant wife Nabanda? A question he could not answer. He remembered well that he was in the process of extending his house. The true fact was that it was not yet his house because through his employers, the Building Society had offered him with a ten-year loan.

Now he was recalling that day he had received the bunch of keys when his excitement was cut short upon realising that the small rooms would not accommodate his family fully. He was extending it now with larger rooms.

But this could not shake off that feeling of why the authorities were targeting him to do this job? Street raids.

This was not his trouble. The City Fathers were the ones at fault in not fulfilling their election promises. The stalls had not been built and now with the economy nose-diving once again and the vendors were always on the streets early and it was from the proceeds of the street sales that food was brought on their table.

"I think I have said enough, do you have any questions Banda!?

"No Sir!" Banda stammered.

"Leave now" "the Superintendent's barking voice echoed in between Banda's big ears. He was out in a flash.

Back in his small stuffy Office Sergeant Major Banda felt dizzy and confused. Somewhere inside his head he felt something like a sharp thorn prickling his brain He was twisting his mind over the task at hand. His pock-marked and rubbery face normally had a touch of humour about the eyes, but now it showed only stubborn determination to succeed in the raid. He was ready now.

In the city pavement Veronica Majasi sat close to a take-way shop, her eyes hovering over her wares. Having lost her husband, Veronica a light brown beautiful lady with two kids to look after now survived on street vending. It was towards lunch time in the city as she took the first sip of a mineral drink. Her mouth felt supple.

Now she watched with amusement at the different pairs of feet passing bye, city men with glittering sharp-pointed shoes, unemployed youth in trendy shoes whose shoelaces hang loosely, and young girls with nothing to do, in fashionable clogs. The occasional rural woman on a first visit to the city walking in torn black tennis shoes, one arm holding to a dirty bag and at one corner of this bag then a protruding towel or was it a napkin, Veronica could not tell.

The woman nevertheless walked on one hand supporting a baby who was fast asleep judging by the hanging head. Momentarily, out of pity Veronica's eyes trailed her. Poor woman she thought to herself, for her ankles where caked with dust the result of walking possibly on a footpath.

"Catch her!" Banda barked in a hoarse piercing voice. Three young municipal guards jumped swiftly from the open truck. Veronica realised it too late. Like a bushbuck cornered by a pack of wild dogs she bobbed her head forwards and backwards to side step the guards and escape, but they could have none of it. One of the guards grabbed her hand and the young woman attempted to wriggle herself free in vain. This caused a sudden stir from lunch time shoppers who watched wares strewn all over the pavements.

"Leave her, hey leave her!" Two touts at a nearby commuter terminus tried to intimidate the guards. Two shots from Banda's pistol silenced them and they disappeared like rats behind commuter omnibuses packed at the rank terminus.

Now hand-cuffed Veronica was forced to jump into the Municipal open truck and driven to Municipal Building.

"Young lady you can talk now", Banda said gleaning at her face as he interrogated her.

"How many times have you been warned not to sell your wares on our pavements, how many times?"

Banda's raised voice echoed from his small Office.

"But... but ... bu..."

"Shut up! You shut up your smelly mouth!" Banda's eyes were mad with anger.

He felt demeaned, being challenged by a young woman.

"Do you have a hawker's license?" Banda shouted like an enraged bull.

The loud shouting coming from Banda's Office echoed through the office corridors.

Superintendent Jumo felt the urgency to find out. What could that be? Who were they? The last thing Superintendent Jumo could not face was to be held responsible for any incidents that would attract Municipal management and disrupt crucial council meetings. He burst out of his office on a run to find the cause of the loud noise. Opening the door he froze. He had come face to face with what he least expected, his cousin Veronica. At home he had urged her to try her luck but to be always vigilant of street raids. Today she was not lucky. Now as Banda poked her fingers on her calling all sorts of names; divorcee, lady of the night, Superintendent Jumo felt pinched and humiliated.

"She will have to pay a fine", Banda growled triumphantly.

Superintendent Jomo's blinking eyes displayed embarrassment and self-pity. Now he could not shout his commanding voice neither could he look at Veronica, directly into her face.

"I will be back" Superintendent Jumo shot out.

"Bandaaa come here!" The booming voice echoed through the long Municipal corridor from the Superintendent's Office.

Banda arrived breathlessly.

"Release the lady now", the Superintendent commanded madly.

"But Senior, why?" Banda attempted to counter him.

"*Iwe*, I said release her now!" The glaring mad eyes were frightening.

Fearing for his job and house Banda removed the handcuffs and set the lady free. "You can go" he told her in a resigned voice.

Veronica opened her mouth in shock. She could not believe what was happening. As she walked along the corridor it felt as if she had been in a prison and had tested her freedom at long last.

Alone reflecting, Banda shook his head. Two months and no salary yet. Back home the family awaited his return. Just a week back a cousin had brought him message of his ailing mother who was longing to see him. He was in the middle of all these thoughts when Superintendent Jumo banged the door open.

"You can go home now" But these words did not placate him. He felt used and abused. Tears almost welled up his eyes. But an inner voice encouraged him to be a man, to hold on and to feel no remorse. With a tired yawn he stretched his big arms, pulled a bunch of keys, looked at his Office for the last time and headed home.

Midnight Parties

I set my foot on the veranda before being ushered into the room to be greeted by glowing bright lights. The lady who ushered me put on an all-white attire, walking on high-hilled stiletto shoes that produced a light tapping sound on the tiled floor. Suddenly, I looked in wonder upon realising that almost everyone in the house was dressed in all white. This made me feel out of place, but before long a light-skinned lady with a crown on her head walked majestically and came to kiss me on my forehead. I felt a throbbing heartbeat beneath my ribcage.

"Welcome to the party of the chosen few, feel at home", she said to me teasingly outstretching her hands with red manicured fingers. She looked at me pleadingly. Oh! Those pair of seductive eyes were eye-catching leaving me with a heavenly feeling.

One of the ushering ladies immediately handed me a glassful of red wine. After taking my first sip my mouth felt supple, eyes opening widely with a new awakening. I felt as if a romantic comfort had gripped me. My head started reeling in circles. Could this be the effects of red wine already taking a tall on me?

Then my glazing eyes became adventurous running around the room, mesmerised by the glistering decorations until they finally rested on the high table. Oblong-shaped draped in white and gold cloth with a variety of wine bottles lined up, my eyes marvelled at this somewhat unique table reserved for the royalty. The upright fans standing a few metres away added to the coolness of the room. I grinned a little with mischief at the effect I felt as the blowing fan lightly caressed my chicks. Goodness me I felt on cloud nine.

Derek my room-mate at our local University had told me of these all-night parties before. Being a novice, I had taken him for granted and dismissed such parties as mere spectacle. But strangely, after reading an open invitation poster now here I was. What had drawn me here?

Taking stock of my surroundings, I despised myself for rushing myself, arriving shabbily dressed. No wonder I felt a loner in the blue jean with holes and a grey long-sleeved shirt borrowed from a friend.

I could observe that the ladies knew better about these parties and came appropriately dressed. They were looking as if they had just been born. With light make-up, red lips and manicured fingers they held their wine glasses with tips of their fingers as if they had been trained movie style. Time and again as they came into contact with familiar friends, they held their glasses high to toast and giggle like children.

The few boys who were present had given me a cold shoulder look. Their disarming looks was enough expression that signalled their mere disgust at my presence. So, I wrapped myself all alone by the corner like a small bundle. Thank God, a very faint background music kept me company.

I was in the middle nestling my glass wine when I felt a light touch on my shoulder.

"Hello Calisto, feel at home, you deserve to be at the high table", The lady host held my hand gently. I felt the strong scent of heavy perfume all over her body that tingled the inner veins of my nostrils as she led me like a sheep to a slaughter. An urge to sneeze almost caught me but I quickly held it back. Then I gazed at her equally heavy make-up on her eyelashes and brow. It reminded me of the biblical Jezebel, that biblical name sent shocking anguish on my whole being.

"Relax Calisto relax, the night is still young", She calmed me and her eyes held mine as if she had read my alarmed feelings. She pulled a chair for me to seat on. Not long one of the lady ushers was breathing by my neck refilling my wine glass. It seemed everything happening around me had been well programmed.

A wild sensation was beginning to overwhelm my body and the hairs on my head felt like rising. My two trembling hands could hardly hold the tiny neck of the wine glass. Nevertheless, I put on a brave face.

A few weeks into college life I had overhead it said on Campus there were secret societies, like drug dealers, gays, parting groups, gamblers and ritualists. A lot of students were being lured and initiated into Satanism unknowingly. Could this be a trap? I was wondering and confused. I had come here to learn and my parents had counselled me not to be involved in activities that would ruin my university education.

Could these be consequences of my action knocking on my door? Only time would tell.

"Calisto the wine, drink up, young man", I almost spilled the contains of my glass as the lady host stared into my eyes with a glowing smile. Surprisingly and in contrast her eyes were wolfish and cunning. Never had I seen such eyes in my life. Dare Devil eyes. I almost shouted a wild cry of horror only to restrain myself. The stakes seemed to be against me now as I felt like a bushbuck surrounded and trapped by a pack of wild dogs.

"Just a minute to the restroom, I will be back", I told the lady host moving away in panic.

By the time I reached the restroom the inner voice that had echoed through my eardrums urging me to escape seemed as if reverberating now. Calisto, run for your life now! Following a passage inside the house I bumped through two boys and seeing an opening took to my heels. For a second I felt as if blind.

I headed towards the valley separating the new location from the University Campus. Running for my dear life along the footpath I could only hear my laboured breathe. Something strange seemed as if moving besides me in the grass. At first, I ignored it dismissing the sensations of my ears. Once or twice, I slowed my run to pick up the weird sound. Before reaching the tarred road, a huge snake appeared right in front of me. The lady host had transformed into a huge snake. It would seem like a dream movie but before taking decisive action, strangely enough, a whirlwind lifted me into the air.

The next moment I found myself running along the tarred road in the dead of the night. Above me the glowing concrete pole lights provided me with enough vision. A light shadow was ahead of me. My own shadow. Turning by the corner, I felt the sharp pain on my head.

"Hold on, hold on, turn him this side", a distance voice cautioned.

"Will he make it?" faintly a voice uttered in panic.

Flashing red lights flooded the place from where I lay. My blurred sight had glimpses of huge black safety shoes, and men's rushing feet. Much later I felt the weight of my whole body being lifted in the air.

"He will live", and those were the last words that registered in my ears as I found myself surrounded by my family members in a brightly lit hospital ward the following morning. Seeing my father's glaring eyes rest upon me sent teardrops of regret running down my chicks. Yes, I was alive, my life had been spared.

The housing stands

The small hall was filled to the entrance. Those with handkerchiefs were waving them in front of their faces to cool off. Despite all their efforts the air remained stable and oppressively hot. All around Vasco were damp and tired faces. A peculiar odour of armpits also pervaded the packed hall. Vasco felt the tingling of his nostrils, almost sneezing. He looked around himself once again. The majority of workers here were cleaners, grounds men, mechanics and workers from the Agriculture and Kitchen Sections. They had left their work sections in haste. They were here to decide their own destiny in matters to do with decent living so was Vasco.

Amid the mumbling voices, everybody waited in anticipation for the arrival of the Ministry Officials for earlier in the day word had been spread to all departments that the meeting for Housing Stands was being convened in the University's Great Hall. Vasco found himself inside the hall with a mission to listen with his own big ears and get the first-hand information, he could not let the chance slip away.

"I heard about it when I was about to dash to the city", the middle-aged woman spoke as she wiped off dripping sweat from her forehead.

"Haha!! You were going to miss this rare opportunity", the other lady putting on a blue uniform chuckled.

Sitting on perforated chairs and feeling comfortable they laughed good-naturedly, their palms clashing in mid-air.

A few metres from where they sat some young men sat closely to each other, deep in conversation. They spoke in hushed tones cupping their mouths making sure that not everybody would catch any word. They had hidden plans. The air around was one of feverish excitement.

Now Vasco's eyes scanned the environment until they focused on the front table. He could pick the familiar faces of the University Union leaders as they sat on chairs behind a large table draped with white cloth. A plastic vase filled with artificial rose flowers occupied the centre of the table. Time and again one of the Union leaders stirred at his wrist watch, always frowning. Could it be that time was not on their side?

Vasco also felt restless now and as he was about to focus on the goings on, he felt a light hand nudge his shoulders.

Turning his head he came face to face with Gilbert from the Bursar's Office.

"How long have you been here, Vasco?", the Accounting Officer asked him with a broad smile. "Twenty minutes", he replied back.

"Aalaa these people never keep time", Gilbert complained.

"Let us wait and see, maybe it's a matter of time", Vasco calmed him. Suddenly the entire hall went silent.

Three men in suits streamed into the Great Hall followed by a young lady in black shiny high heels that lifted her figure high. She waved them to occupy the front table right in front of the anxious University workers.

The issue of housing stands backlog has been a thorn in the flesh for the government. In the City of Gweru whilst the city fathers had attempted to address it through different high density locations some ten years had lapsed leaving many people still on the waiting list. The coming in of new stakeholders like UNKI Mine, Sino and of the new University knocking on the doors of city fathers to assist their employees afford decent housing had seen them engaging the central government. Now the Ministry officials had made it clear that today they had come in to address this quest for decent housing.

"We have a new scheme coming up along Harare Road so we have approached University authorities to engage you", the short Ministry official announced with a broad smile. It was met with a thunderous applause.

"Once we get the list of potential beneficiaries, we will receive them and advise them of the procedure to follow" the Ministry official concluded before taking his seat.

The news of securing new stands was a welcome relief.

"This is what we have been waiting for all these long years", an elderly man hissed glowering with excitement. Before trickling out of the hall, after the Ministry officials had left, the Union leaders once again reminded the workers to ensure that their names, including employment numbers were captured in their respective Departments.

Late on a Friday, Vasco had overheard a list of potential beneficiaries that had been submitted to the Ministry. Being a Friday, he was preparing to go home early, so he decided to check with the Secretary. Strange! His name was missing.

Taking no further chances, Vasco decided to act now for he knew the situation at hand. At the University Main Gate, he got a lift into town. An hour later he was at the Ministry Offices amongst a crowd of eager stand-seekers. They all held application forms

"Am from the University and my name is not on the list, how come," Vasco fumed.

"Get to the next door, follow the queue and fill your details on the register and get an application form," This was sweet music to his ears

Barely a few minutes later a lady emerged with forms that she handed on. Vasco quickly grabbed one from her. He sat on a bench, an air of relief sweeping all over him. Could it be that he was picturing himself as a proud owner of a new piece of land?

"Move please!!" He felt a slight shove.

Big Vasco found himself seated before a big mahogany table about to enter all his details. At first because of the feverish excitement his big hands felt stiff as if he had suddenly developed arthritic. Then for a moment his heart almost burst with shock imagining that the fingers were about to betray him at the very last crucial moment.

"Go to the next office and pay the initial deposit" the lady secretary advised him.

Vasco left the office and the Ministry of Housing and Amenities premises with the receipt safely tacked on his right pocket, a receipt that would give him proof to pay for his initial deposit. A huge smile beamed for at long last it had dawned to him that he would soon own his own stand.

A week later the news was on the headlines.

"Potential home seekers trapped in a land dispute" read the headline in a local daily.

Vasco could not believe his eyes as he held his head in disbelief. He felt his hairs rising, arms sweaty and shivering. Surely this was not fair at all. All this done right in the front of university authorities. Standing there, his head was running in circles, the world turning against him.

The stakes were against him. He had not told his wife about the money. Where would he find the replacement money to secure his child's Form 1 place? And the School had insisted on full amount. He had taken a gamble. A daring fit. That whole night he remained awake his head cupped in his hands. Time would tell!

Daring chances

Half way through the month of September, Bigboy Mutiro had not received his overtime allowances. So how did the customs authorities expect him to adequately feed and clothe his family back home? It eked him to be treated this way considering the years of service he had sacrificed himself to the job. Today he had not been outdoors and had spent the better part of the day relaxing on his chair to allow his juniors to handle both the incoming and outgoing trucks.

That he had taken the liberty to loosen his muscles was an understatement, the ill treatment had all day been unnerving him. At long last, it was just around midday that he lifted his weighty body from the black chair at the same time, outstretching his arms and yawning. There was a groaning and rumbling sound coming from the pit of his bowels suggesting an empty stomach. A second thought told him he had not taken an early meal. Never mind Bigboy Mutiro focused his attention on the lining trucks stretching for a distance of fifty meters from the Zambian border side.

The white truck passing through the gate from the Zambian side looked fairly new. This caught his eyes. Who could be the owner of this new acquisition? He thought to himself. Hardly a minute later, a tall stocky man wearing a leather cowboy hat dropped from the heavy truck after killing the engine. This he did just a few moments upon passing customs checkpoint, in response to one of the bald-headed customs officer's raised arms signalling him to stop. Bigboy waved his hand in a gesture to advise his junior officer to return back to the office.

Now as he walked gingerly towards this new truck, he could feel his huge distended belly sagging sideways. He was moving boisterously with an air of authority all around him. Step by step bidding his time. Why hurry? Bigboy's nostrils felt the powerful penchant odour of tobacco smoke from the man ahead of him. He almost sneezed his nose releasing some pale white mucus which he wiped with the back of his right arm. What could he have done without a handkerchief?

As he got closer, he cupped his right arm just above his eyes to get a better view of the red number plates. That this was a Democratic Republic of Congo haulage truck could not be begrudged. It appeared obvious to him that this truck could be carrying expensive cargo. His mouth salivated suddenly. Such new trucks had to pay customs duty the moment they entered the borders of Zimbabwe, starting here at Chirundu Border Post.

'Truck from DRC?' Big Mutiro roared loudly. His tone of voice had a hint of authority in its trail.

'Kinshasa to be precise' the truck driver responded, his voice oozing with confidence, never mind his opposite number's bellicose attitude.

'Hmmmmm destination?', again Big Mutiro asked hastily just in case he would catch him off guard.

'Joburg, South Africa *mambo wangu'*, the DRC truck driver responded with a broad smile, perhaps hoping his slight knowledge of the local vernacular language would cheer up the Officer.

Ignoring the response, Bigboy Mutiro narrowed his eyes, noting the plate number once again. He scratched his head as if summoning some thoughts. At the back of his mind, he knew how to deal with these foreign drivers knowing that they would spring a surprise with their bags of tricks. So, he put on a mean and business-like appearance imagining perhaps this would keep this foreign driver at bay.

Bigboy focused his attention at this DRC truck and at the same time playfully caressing his chin. He had a counter book with ZIMRA Logo, at any time he would pick the branded ballpoint from his right ear lobe and start receipting. Could he climb and check on the trailer or just let go? He thought of his huge weight. Various options wrestled in his mind, some drifting on the verge to let go, but being a professional he was he puffed and punted as he hefted his body twice if not thrice before landing inside the truck trailer. For a good minute he gasped to gather back his breath. For some seconds he tried to remember the last time he had been to the gym.

That was an issue for another day. 'Focus'. Was it a hissing voice? He allowed his eyes to run through the length and breadth of this long trailer. He had hardly considered his next step when the truck driver surprisingly landed inside with ease. Rows of plain timber lay from one end of the trailer to the other. With an effort he lifted one.

He nearly fainted with shock. Bigboy sat back and cultivated in himself the spirit of quiet dignity that would be necessary to confront the foreign driver with professionalism. There in front of him were coils of neatly concealed copper cables and other several bags of cement and wall finishing plaster. He felt his heartbeat throbbing as he weighed his next action.

Could he act now and charge a heavy fine? Contrasting thoughts were hovering across his mind. As he bent down, he felt a light hand touch his thick sweaty left arm. Turning gradually his eyes opened widely with shock as they came face to face with a thick bundle of US dollar notes. Black out? For a few seconds it seemed a dark cloud had enveloped him.

Where was he? What!!! In a court of law? He was being cross examined with thousand eyes fixed on him. 'You will be charged for breaking customs regulations by accepting bribes', a man in black robes announced. No!! he had not experienced a brief nightmare. It was not him being charged. That brief spell hardly lasted five minutes and he found himself trembling.

Shell shocked he had to swallow an imaginary lump that had developed on his throat making it impossible for him to utter words. Confusion enveloped him now. Taking a bribe was the last thing that he would dare attempt, but a tempting voice kept echoing to his ear for how could he let go this opportunity. It was this voice that he was following.

'Let's get into the passenger compartment, quick!!' He ordered with a raised voice.

'Fast hey! He implored further. Inside the cabin, not long another thick wad of two thousand US dollar notes exchanged hands quickly. His palms had been greased. His hands shaking, he shoved the fresh bundles of notes inside his underwear. He had been bribed.

'Now drive away immediately and be out of sight', he hissed.

A feeling of guilty conscience troubled him and he felt sweat slid down his spine. His chest was heaving as if under an asthma attack.

'Where is the truck from and heading', the junior officer's question hit him surprisingly.

'Must be a truck of a high-profile politician heading South Africa, all papers were in order', Mutiro lied.

'Where is the evidence?' The question was uttered, suddenly taking Bigboy of guard.

He was seized by sudden anger that made his blood boil. He could have put this junior officer in his place with one word, but on second thoughts he restrained himself. Better play it safe. He cautioned himself. Still feeling the pain of a question from a junior officer on his chest, Mutiro maintained his composure as ever. He told himself never to appear suspicious. No. Bigboy could not allow himself to be cornered by a man his junior.

'I think I feel an upset tummy', Mutiro told his subordinates as he headed to the restroom.

The two junior officers stared at each other in awe as their boss brushed them aside. For ten minutes he fought hard to conceal the money. Now he was feeling the bouncing heartbeat. The last thing he would not figure out would be being accused of corruption. After leaving for home at the end of his shift that night he could not find sleep. Each time he felt for the new notes his heartbeat intensified. Even the thought of being apprehended and made to stand before a court hearing and sent to jail heightened his fears. He hatched the plan. He was not reporting back to work as he had to attend a funeral. That day he had lost his ethics with this unforgivable lie.

Grabbing the canvas bag early at the break of dawn Bigboy shoved himself into the packed car. He had committed the greatest sin, and if there was a heaven he surely would not enter through the gates.

'Gentlemen I trust you have little money enough for your ride', the words from the driver jerked Bigboy with a sickening thoughts. The last thing that was occupying his mind was how he would get rid of the money as soon as he arrived at this rural home. Mentally he had calculated and concluded that the money would be enough to secure him four herds of cattle. So, his heart had leapt, but upon realising he had old notes on his breast pocket despite feeling a slight dampness of his forehead, he handed the driver his dues. Two days later he felt at ease as he headed back to the city. He had even been surprised at the swiftness of the transactions with monies changing hands in the eerie night back at his rural home. There was no sense of pride there. The pride of being a new owner of healthy cattle. What shocked him upon his return back to work was the ease with which they welcomed him, as if he was back from a foreign trip. Yet his guilty conscience continued to gnaw him for he had become the prisoner of his own conscience.

Midnight Neighbourhood Watch

"**S**tandaaa at ease!", the pant-sized Police Officer hissed at our silhouetted figures as we stood akimbo outside Nehanda Police Post, the floodlight a few metres away from us. Eleven o'clock in the late evening night was not the right time for married men with families to protect at home to be here, this odd hour. Circumstances beyond our control had forced us to be here. We had made our decision. It was a bold decision.

In the neighbourhood, a spate of robberies had been reported but no action had been taken. Families had lost valuables like twenty litre plastic buckets, washing dishes, plastic chairs and hoes and shovels. The one that sent tongues wagging was the daring thief who lifted a huge pot with steaming trotters and ran away.

It was the talk of the whole neighbourhood for weeks. So, the men of the neighbourhood had decided that enough was enough.

'Attention!', Kheda the Police Officer barked instructions catching us off guard. As family men we had freely volunteered and sacrificed to be trained here at this parade. We followed the barking orders stamping our feet unevenly. However, with time we found the right and perfect rhythm henceforth we all responded simultaneously, stamping our feet to the ground heavily and in unison.

I found myself intrigued by this Police Officer who made us sweat with the drills. Standing one-and-half feet and light in complexion, one would be forgiven to assume that he was of a coloured descent, but amazingly he barked his instructions in fluent local Shona vernacular language.

"I will hand you over to Sergeant Mzondiwa, have you heard me *varume*?" He announced in a commanding and forceful voice that sounded as if to compensate for his small stature. It had high authority in it that took the tall mature elderly men in front of me off guard. I almost guffawed.

'Shef Muzondiwa will be your leader and guide in this operation you are about to embark on, understand!' He shouted loudly as if enlisting our maximum cooperation.

Today I was going through an experience I least expected. The urge to giggle almost seized me but an inner fear restrained me and did not allow my excited nerves to get the better of me. I observed every step he took. It was calculated. Maybe I was mistaken, he wanted just to exploit this opportunity to show off in front of us? Why not, after all this was his turf. He was in charge of course.

To divert these aching thoughts from my mind I forced myself to look back when earlier that morning we had gathered by the popular neighbourhood kiosk and invited police details to hear our plight.

Reflecting on the particular day, the neighbourhood people had responded overwhelmingly. Women who bore the brunt of thefts came wrapped in Zambian cloth around their waists.

They then sat on the ground. One of their own volunteered to deliver an opening prayer. Thereafter, it was the turn of the appointed Chairperson to invite the few Police Officers who had turned up to address us. One of them who had a crop of white hair cleared his throat and wiped his patched lips.

'The decision is yours to come up with a formidable team to constitute your neighbourhood patrol', remarked the tired looking Police Officer after first of all feeding our tired minds with Police Acts and Regulations for the better part of an uninterrupted hour. He even mentioned talk of vetting us at the Police Station.

Our neighbourhood area was an extension of newly built houses by a local Bank in the City of Gweru. This being my third year stay in this neighbourhood what was most disturbing were the sudden break-ins. Worst of all reports of daylight break-ins were happening in houses where families were out at their workplaces. With nightfall under cover of darkness daring thieves targeted houses with Satellite dishes.

With the economy bringing breadwinners to their knees, with little income to put food on the table after closure of local industries, it seemed to the unemployed and retrenched thrived on thievery. Their last option for survival. They considered hitting these University employees where it hurt most, their gadgets like computers, laptops, and the latest iPads, and Smartphones. Having been one such victim and it hurt me badly.

It was whilst my mind was lost in these thoughts that Kheda barked again with heightened authority bringing me back to my senses.

I stood to attention.

'I am informed by Sergeant Mzondiwa that you have come up with your Neighbourhood Watch. Am I right?'

He turned his head this way and that way in a mocking gesture as if soliciting for answers from everyone one of us.

'You will be operating under the name "The Jericho Walls Brigade Neighbourhood Watch.', get that right. He reiterated

Twelve midnight saw us leaving the environs of the Nehanda Police Station, setting off towards our neighbourhood, more determined than before in this eerie night.

All was quiet in the High-Density Suburb, serve for a few barking dogs here and there. From a distance we could hear the sound of a braying donkey. Perhaps it had caught a cold, I surmised and almost giggled to the taught.

Ahead of us our Patrol Commander putting on a flat faded Police cap and an aerial cell phone in hand walked bullishly his head sticking forward. Time and again he would listen to the audible messages that constantly interrupted him each time he attempted to brief us on tactics to use upon encountering any loitering persons.

Nevertheless, I could see that he was putting on airs around him by the way he walked and the inflated authority he assumed.

'Right gentlemen, right now we will head towards the Shopping Centre'

'Are we together?' He swerved backwards, casting glances to register whether we were still on the same page.

'We will close all the beer halls and nightclubs and force the night revellers to go home'.

'Close the beerhalls?' I felt shocked to hear him talk about this high-handed authority. How would the revellers react to such a sudden instruction at the prime of their happiness? The revellers were enjoying the heavy disco music and drowning their sorrows. I just imagined what their reaction would be.

The lead officer walked bobbing his head. I frowned at him in the dark as I felt disgusted by his arrogance.

I felt for my small notebook and pen tucked in my leather jacket. Not long we cornered two lovebirds.

'Good evenings kindly produce your identity cards', the tall arrogant Police Officer instructed them.

'Your first name?' I asked the male who was partially drunk.

'Gilbert Madora' was the curt reply.

'Your house address', I followed up.

The man staggered backwards almost loosing balance. He muttered inaudible sounds taking long to construct words.

We left him leaning on a Durawall.

Not long we entered the small bar where family men were enjoying themselves what to their standard deemed to be quality time. Inside the humid beerhall I felt the chocking mixture of beer and cigarette smell and withdraw outside.

We left our lead officer attending to the bartender. They took a while to exchange conversations. It was getting late, and one by one the bar patrons were leaving.

"Time to move on in separate ways" the Officer gave the clue. So, in trio we went on our separate ways.

"Thieves", the high-pitched voice of sergeant Muzondiwa echoed in the silent neighboured.

We all sprang into action heading towards him. Two men with potbellies had outpaced me and upon my arrival on the scene they were panting bending and holding on to their waists.

"They were three thieves, with dark masks heavily armed with machetes", Muzondiwa announced.

"Who of you would have had dared approach them", sergeant Muzondiwa grinned in our faces beneath the glowing summer moon.

Would we take him for his word? Or was this all this an attempt to test our vigilance on this very first patrol?

"That's all for this first hurdle, lets head home"

With these parting words we headed each on our separate ways home as the first cock crow registered in our ears.

Christmas comes once in a blue moon.

Today the streets are crowded with an air of suppressed excitement. It is probably because the world remittances had arrived from distance relatives in the Diaspora. Hence these weary faced Zimbabwean men, women, young boys and girls wait in bated breath to get their chance to get inside the *Mukuru* Money Transfer agency.

Amid this excitement there is a mass of human movement with shoulders brushing against each other. Domingo watched as the crowd squeezed and elbowed each other in an attempt to be the first to be served.

This awkward behaviour immediately prompted him to instinctively feel for his right breast pocket. For some couple of seconds, the throbbing heart beneath his ribcage had alarmed him. Soon his worst fear had abated as he felt a thickness of leaves of money thrusted deep inside his right pocket. Satisfied a broad smile swept across his face. He could have shouted bravo! Instead, he just giggled at the thought.

Domingo knew he had to send the money as soon as possible. Suddenly a tall ganglier young man emerged

"Ten people move in," the young man announced as he opened the door.

That's when the pandemonium began.

"You, woman in Chitenge cloth, you jumped the queue", a woman a few metres back voiced anger. The farrows on her forehead had thickened. She was visibly angry finding it hard to hold her breath.

'You won't get in there otherwise we will cause trouble', the other women behind joined in.

All attempts for the woman to reason with the young man for some favours were fruitless. They remained standing there as the other people trickled inside the Mukuru agency. We looked on.

"What's going on today, huhh?" An elderly woman complained behind Domingo.

"We are here to send money and you keep us waiting," she raised her voice now.

We did not come here to make numbers we want to deposit money and leave', another elderly woman fumed wiping beads of sweat on her forehead.

There were some murmuring voices amid the tense atmosphere almost getting out of hand. Fearing abuse, a young lady retreated back inside the agency hall.

Passing police details stood momentarily to gather the cause of the apprehension before disappearing. The woman vendor who had wrapped his tiny merchandise in a worn out filthy black sack with long strings was soon back. Domingo shook his head pitying the women. Her kind were those women who played hide and seek with both Municipal Police and Police Constables, on a daily basis. It was here at the end of the city area called… 'The Third World, a favourite hunting ground for hustlers, thieves, vendors of all shapes and sizes where the majority of the poor survived on hustling.

Domingo felt a nudge on his shoulder.

'Time to move in elder', the young lady smiled at him. Moments later he is inside the Mukuru agency. Domingo could see the orange coat and sparkling Christmas decorations on the counters.

'On the floor you will see some black marks, please parents let's observe social distancing', the young lady advised in a light-hearted voice.

"Also, there are some of you who have jumped the queue entering inside without being sanitised. Shall we go outside please", she warned before inspecting the palms. Even before the suspects were identified a furious woman had courageously offered to identify them.

'Your national identity please', the lady on the counter hissed to Domingo's ear.

'And eee how much are you sending' the woman half stammered

"US$90.00 please', Domingo replied fishing the identity card from inside the right pocket of his jacket. Having retrieved the money, he felt a glowing breath of fresh air like as if a heavy load has been lifted off his shoulders.

Back in the streets he weaved his way avoiding pavement vendors selling school shoes, uniforms and writing books.

Across the main street close to a popular supermarket milling customers readied to enter shoving and elbowing each other. Mealie meal had arrived and everyone longed to grab a sack. Domingo arrived just in time and happily joined the queue and grab this opportunity for Christmas came once in a blue. Grinning to the thought he waited with patience for his turn to be ushered in.

Workers' Union goes to the polls

After almost two years of waiting, the Electoral College finally met and decided on the date of the Election. The news gripped the Olomo University workers with feverish excitement for they had painstakingly waited for this day. Two posts were at stake, the President of the University Workers' Union and the Secretary General. Whom would they vote for to occupy these posts? Who would contest to win the elections? The workers waited in anticipation.

Early next morning the university workers woke up to see the election date and campaign posters with images of aspiring candidates.

Tinboy Njuga announced that he was in the race to contest for the vacant post for the President post, for a third term. His message boasted that his past experience was enough to leverage him to be capable of resolving compelling issues affecting workers' welfare. But who would be willing to listen to him? The question in many workers' minds pertained to the countless blunders during his two terms in office. Allegations of him being a tool of university authorities to undermine workers' grievances were still fresh in the minds of many as well.

The other candidate, Kedha Mukiwa, once a workers' representative in the University Council had joined the race. His message was that it was the right time to grab the

Presidency post and lead the suffering University workers and resolve their understanding grievances once and for all. Always putting on a good-natured smile, openly used his brief Election Manifesto as his trump card to campaign. Some University employees candidly called him "Our Mukiwa" because of his light complexion. He was promising to bring a new order by ushering in a professionally disciplined new leadership.

The diminutive Maxim Giant outgoing Secretary General was daring to retain his post. As an administrator on university workers' chat group, he used this platform to remind them not to forget him as that tried and tested cadre who would take their concerns to the University authorities fearlessly. He also boosted knowing every high Office and the right channels to reach responsible authorities without fear or favour. Of course there were other candidates campaigning from the peripherals, but these three were the most outspoken and displayed their hunger for the two big posts at their disposal. They showed their immense zeal through the campaign messages appearing on the University Staff's chat group at every hour.

"Whom does Tinboy think he will hoodwink this time around", the toothless Domingo gestured to his colleague as they waited for the University bus shuttle to arrive.

"Colleagues I will not be that dump to vote for him again", hissed Piyo with a frown.

"Two terms without a financial statement huh! What is that?" Piyo now burst out angrily.

"You can imagine what kind of a leader we would endure if we make the mistake of voting him back into Office", Dimongo replied back hoping to hear his friend's response only to be met with Piyo's red eyes. Piyo was one of those unfortunate victims of a botched housing scheme. They had been promised stands after paying huge sums of money, only to be swindled without any compensation. The more he thought of it the angrier he became. It was all because of Tinboy Njuga.

Friday morning dark clouds hang in the sky presenting a gloomy outlook. At the former Administration Building just close to where the nation's flag is hoisted a group of campus security were milling around. One by one, personnel from the offices of different offices came out. Hanging around, they spoke in whispers.

"Look there those security officers have come in their numbers to vote for their own", Moleen told her friend.

Mr Agrippa Manyuwa had been campaigning on the workers' chat group for the post of Secretary General so his workmates came to vote for him. However, it had been gathered from the grapevine that the security officers were due to attend a Workshop, this being true so they had sneaked out to vote early and then attend the Workshop.

When the truck carrying ballot boxes arrived it did not take long for university workers to line up to cast their vote. There were three polling stations, this being the first.

It takes two weeks for the results to be announced on the workers' group chat.

However, the Electoral College advised the results were yet to be made official. What could be the delay?

"We here that the election results will not be announced until further notice", said one of the members of the Electoral College.

I happened to pass through one of the offices when this latest development came within my earshot. Suddenly I was in the midst of a serious hushed discussion.

"They want to impose their own, a stooge who bends to their rules", an irate voice could be heard.

"But our own is holding his stand", said another voice confidently.

The University workers waited in vain. The results could not be officially published and the winning candidate had not been given the seal of approval to lead the University Worker's Union.

The disgruntled workers could on mill around confused and agitated. What would be the next option. Perhaps opt for the Labour Court. Weeks, months passed. Would there be a hearing? Would the Union Committee be fully complemented. Only time would tell.

Mmap Fiction and Drama Series

If you have enjoyed *The Kule Tokwe Diaries* consider these other fine books in **Mmap Fiction and Drama Series** from *Mwanaka Media and Publishing:*

The Water Cycle by Andrew Nyongesa

A Conversation..., A Contact by Tendai Rinos Mwanaka

A Dark Energy by Tendai Rinos Mwanaka

Keys in the River: New and Collected Stories by Tendai Rinos Mwanaka

How The Twins Grew Up/Makurire Akaita Mapatya by Milutin Djurickovic and Tendai Rinos Mwanaka

White Man Walking by John Eppel

The Big Noise and Other Noises by Christopher Kudyahakudadirwe

Tiny Human Protection Agency by Megan Landman

Ashes by Ken Weene and Umar O. Abdul

Notes From A Modern Chimurenga: Collected Struggle Stories by Tendai Rinos Mwanaka

Another Chance by Chinweike Ofodile

Pano Chalo/Frawn of the Great by Stephen Mpashi, translated by Austin Kaluba

Kumafulatsi by Wonder Guchu

The Policeman Also Dies and Other Plays by Solomon A. Awuzie

Fragmented Lives by Imali J Abala

In the Beyond by Talent Madhuku

Zororo Risina Zororo by Oscar Gwiriri

Sword of Vengeance by Olatubosun David

Finding A Way Home by Tendai Mwanaka

Your Epistle by Solomon A Awuzie

The Restless Run and Ruin of the Roaches and Rats by McLayode

The Reign of Terror by Ntando Gerald

Ibala Lyabwina Nama by Austin Kaluba

Daddy, Please Don't Kill Mama by Natisha Parsons

Pilate's Angels by Goodenough Mashego

Blue threads and other stories by Matthew Kunashe Chikono

The Sylvia Plath Effect by Abigail George

The Twins by Shakemore Dirani

I, Robert's Robot and other stories by Marvel Chukwudi Pephel

Conversation With My Mother by Wonder Guchu

Stranger In Her Own Skin by William Mpina

Zimbolicious 10th Anniversary, Fictions by Tendai Rinos Mwanaka

Soon to be released

https://facebook.com/MwanakaMediaAndPublishing/